THE BONE STRANGER

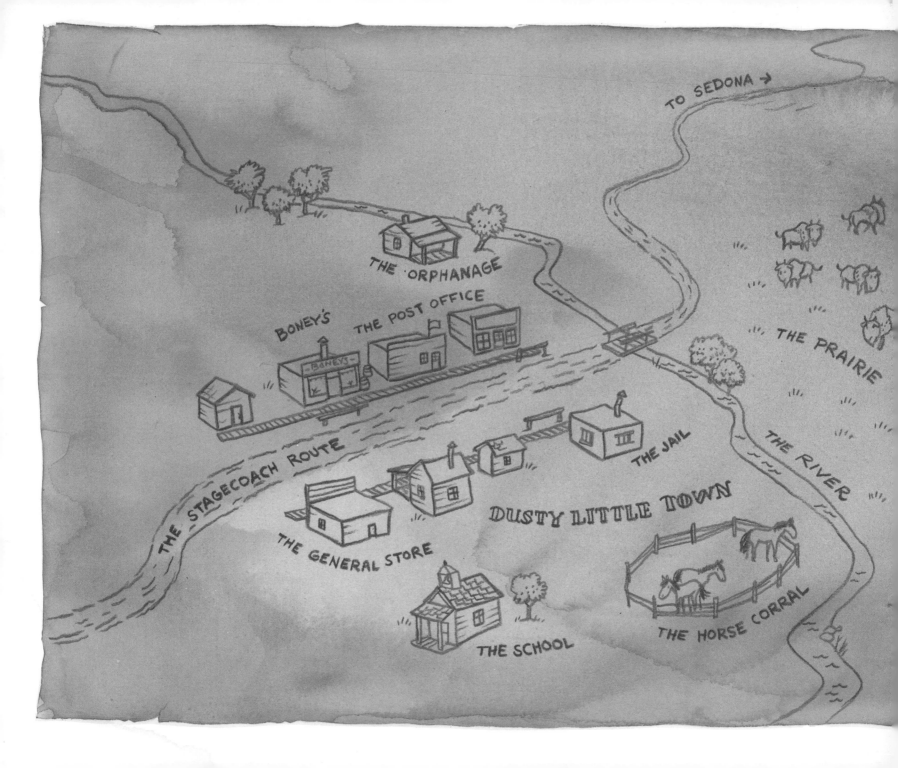

THE BONE STRANGER

Frank Remkiewicz

WHERE THE
BUFFALO ROAM

THE BADLANDS

Lothrop, Lee & Shepard Books

New York

For Joe Giordiano

First Edition   1   2   3   4   5   6   7   8   9   10

Library of Congress Cataloging in Publication
Remkiewicz, Frank. The bone stranger / by Frank Remkiewicz
p.   cm.   Summary: The Bone Stranger and his faithful companion Wolfgang ride to the rescue when the Raccoon
Brothers hold up the stage and steal the orphans' doggie bones. ISBN 0-688-12041-5. —ISBN 0-688-12042-3 (lib. bdg.)
[1. Dogs—Fiction.   2. West (U.S.)—Fiction.]   I. Title.   PZ7.R2835Bo   1994   [E]—dc20   93-25214   CIP   AC

In the days of the wild and woolly west, in a dusty little town on the prairie, was a delicatessen called Boney's. Boney made the fluffiest egg salad, the spiciest corned beef, the tastiest bagels, and the richest, most full-bodied coffee in the territory. Refills were free.

Of course, no dog could do all of this alone. By Boney's side, through dust storms and gully washers, was his faithful companion, Wolfgang. While he practiced speaking English, Wolfgang washed the dishes, swept and mopped the floor, and made the strudel.

Between the breakfast crowd
and the lunch crowd, while Boney
and Wolfgang exercised in back of
the deli, the citizens of the little
town went about their chores and
waited for Saturday, when they
would all gather for the arrival of
the stagecoach.

So there they all were, in front of the post office, on the
Saturday when Big Trouble rolled into town in a cloud of
gritty dust.

"We've been robbed!" yelled the driver. "The Raccoon
Brothers stole the strongbox that was coming to the
orphanage!"

"Oh, no!" cried the young widow who took care of the orphans. "That strongbox was full of doggie bones for the children's bedtime snacks!" The orphans began to cry.

The widow was very pretty, even when she was upset. Boney felt a tug at his heart. "Can I get you a cup of coffee?" he asked. "Or perhaps some lemonade?"

"You can get me the sheriff!" cried the widow. "Where's the sheriff?"

"I think he's in Sedona, visiting his grandmother," said Boney. "I have some nice sticky buns, or perhaps you'd prefer a cinnamon roll?"

"Someone must *do* something!" moaned the widow. But with the sheriff gone, no one knew what to do.

"Raccoon Brothers very bad fellas," said Wolfgang back
at the deli.

"Indeed they are," replied Boney. "*We* have to do something
about this." He scribbled a list. "Go to the general store,
Wolfgang, then to the horse corral. Get everything on this
list. Then meet me behind the deli tonight."

"Ja, Boney!" said Wolfgang, and he slipped out the door
like a shadow on his secret mission.

That night, with no bedtime snack, the orphans were cranky and couldn't get to sleep. But they weren't the only ones who were awake.

As the moon rose above the prairie, Wolfgang returned
to the deli with *almost* all the items on the list.
Boney looked at the horses. "Are they fast?" he asked.

"Very fast!" said Wolfgang. "This big white fella, name
Sauerkraut. Smell kinda funny, but go good with hot dogs.
Other horse name Spot. Also very fast."

The disguises on the shopping list worked well. "No one will recognize us now," said Boney. "But where are the lassos?"

"No lassos," said Wolfgang. "Three stores, all fresh out."

"We'll have to use our jump ropes, then," said Boney.
"Now get the hard salamis and let's ride!"

They tiptoed the horses to the edge of the slumbering town, then thundered across the moonlit prairie, stopping only to sniff for clues.

Finally Wolfgang found the trail. "Raccoon Brothers look
for water, Boney." The trail led across the river, but there
was no sign that the two bandits had stopped. "Not stay here,
Boney, too close to town."

So into the badlands they rode. The ground was parched and barren except for spiny cactus. No creatures roamed here, not even buffalo.

Clever Wolfgang was headed for the Last Chance water hole. Boney felt a tingle of excitement and danger. Beneath the disguise his fur stood on end. He knew they were close!

They drew their salamis, held
the jump ropes in their teeth, and
silently crept closer to the water
hole. Doggie-bone crumbs were
scattered all around, and there
were strange sounds in the night.

"Raccoon snoring," whispered
Wolfgang.

Boney nodded as they crawled
forward, squinting through the
darkness.

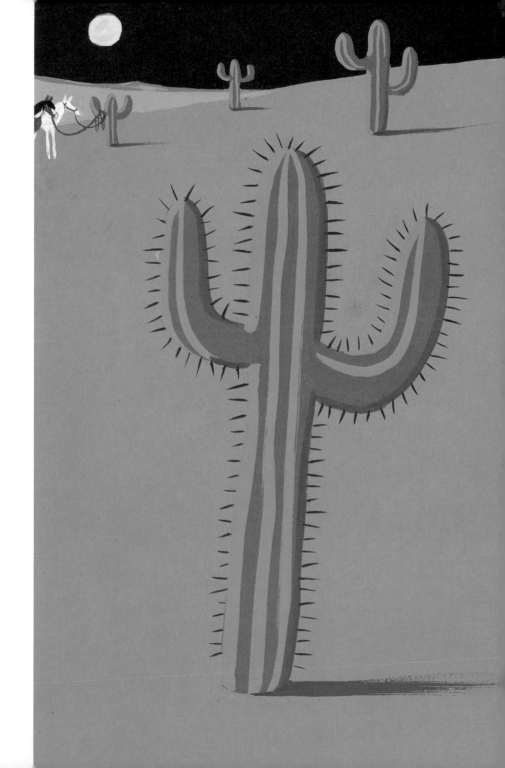

Sure enough, there behind a pile of boulders were the Raccoon
Brothers, fast asleep, their bellies fat with stolen bedtime
snacks. The lightning-fast attack caught the sleepy scoundrels by
surprise. Before they could even scratch or burp, they were tied
up with jump ropes and bundled onto the great horse, Sauerkraut.

The long night was getting shorter, but Boney and Wolfgang managed to get in a little rope jumping as they vamoosed back to town, where they locked the Raccoon Brothers in jail, then delivered the almost full strongbox to the orphanage.

The weary orphans ate their snack, then dropped into their beds and fell fast asleep.

"It's a miracle," cried the young widow as the two heroes leaped onto their horses and rode off into the glow of dawn. "Who is that masked dog?"

"Why, that must be the Bone Stranger!" said her helper, the oldest orphan. Then the two of them shared a doggie bone and went to bed themselves.

EPILOGUE

Boney and Wolfgang got back to the deli just in time to shed their costumes, toast the bagels, and brew coffee for the breakfast crowd.

Wolfgang was so exhausted, there was no strudel for a whole week.

When the sheriff stepped off the stagecoach the following Saturday, he found two robbers in his jail.

That evening, Boney left a tray of sticky buns on the widow's doorstep.

On Sunday, the sheriff returned from his morning walk to find the Raccoon Brothers gone, the stovepipe disconnected, and black sooty footprints all over the roof.

The widow found an empty silver sandwich tray on her doorstep and black sooty footprints that led off toward the Badlands.